STILL MORE STORIES TO SOLVE

STILL MORE STORIES TO SOLVE

FOURTEEN FOLKTALES FROM AROUND THE WORLD

TOLD BY
GEORGE SHANNON

ILLUSTRATED BY
PETER SÍS

A BEECH TREE PAPERBACK BOOK
NEW YORK

The Library of Congress
has cataloged the Greenwillow Books edition
of *Still More Stories to Solve* as follows:
Shannon, George.
Still more stories to solve :
fourteen folktales from around the world /
told by George Shannon ; pictures by Peter Sís.
p. cm.
Includes bibliographical references.
Summary: Fourteen brief folktales in which there is a
mystery or problem that the reader is invited to solve
before the resolution is presented.
ISBN 0-688-04619-3
1. Tales. [1. Folklore. 2. Literary recreations.] I. Sís,
Peter, ill. II. Title. PZ8.1.S49Sr 1994 398.21—dc20
[E] 93-26529 CIP AC

1 3 5 7 9 10 8 6 4 2
First Beech Tree Edition, 1996
ISBN 0-688-14743-7

WITH THANKS TO ALL
WHO GARDEN
ANCIENT TALES

CONTENTS

INTRODUCTION

People throughout the world know the power of words. Words can spark a smile or cut like broken glass. They can soothe or insult, explain or create confusion. At times one word can change everything, but other times all the words in the world are not enough to make things change. Everyone has felt the delight of finding new ways to use or interpret a familiar word.

Words also tell our stories. The tales shared here all hinge on the way we use words. Like poets, some characters use or interpret words in fresh, surprising ways. Others discover they should have listened or spoken more carefully. And a few experience the power of words that come straight from the heart. By reading and listening to the ways these characters use words, readers will be able to solve the stories gathered here.

1.
THE LINE

*B*irbal was jester, counselor, and fool to the great Moghul emperor, Akbar. The villagers loved to talk of Birbal's wisdom and cleverness, and the emperor loved to try to outsmart him.

One day Akbar, the emperor, drew a line across the floor.

"Birbal," he ordered, "you must make this line shorter. But you cannot erase any bit of it!"

Everyone present thought the emperor had finally found a way to outsmart Birbal. It was clearly an impossible task. Yet within moments the emperor and everyone present had to agree that Birbal had made the line shorter without erasing any part of it. How could this be?

HOW IT WAS DONE

Birbal simply drew a longer
line next to the first one—
which made the first line
shorter than the second.

2.

TWO HORSES

*T*here was once a king who had two sons. When he grew old and close to death, he sent for his sons.

"I want you to ride your horses to Jerusalem. The one whose horse arrives last will inherit everything I own."

The two princes mounted their horses. But, since each knew his horse had to arrive last if he was to win, both sons rode as slowly as they possibly could. One was forever trying to lag behind the other. When they finally reached the outskirts of Jerusalem, both sons stopped. Neither dared go a step closer for fear of getting there first and thus letting the other one arrive last and inherit the kingdom.

They sat for a day. Then two. They sat for a week and began to feel as if they'd spend the rest of their lives sitting at the edge of Jerusalem with nothing to their names. Then, suddenly, both sons had the same idea. They each jumped on a horse and rode to Jerusalem as fast as they could go. What made them change their minds and find a way to end the competition?

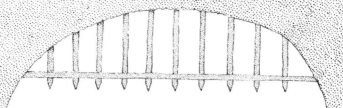

HOW IT WAS DONE

Each jumped on his brother's horse to finish the race. If one could ride the other's horse to the city first, it meant his own horse would arrive last and *he* would inherit the kingdom.

3.

NEVER
SET FOOT

Long ago in Ethiopia there lived a man named Abunawas who was famous for his cleverness. One day the emperor made him a guard, and trouble was frequent from that point on. No matter what the emperor told him to do, Abunawas was able to find a way out of doing it.

When he wanted to go dancing, for example, after being ordered to watch the palace gate, Abunawas simply took the gate with him where he went to dance.

One day the emperor got so angry he told Abunawas he never wanted to see his face again. But this only created new problems. After that, when the emperor passed by, it meant Abunawas could turn around and bow with his seat to the emperor instead of the respectful way with his face.

The emperor finally got so angry he ordered Abunawas to leave the country.

"You can go anywhere," said the emperor. "But if you ever set foot on Ethiopian soil again, I'll have your life!"

The other people of the palace had enjoyed Abunawas's cleverness and were sad to see him go. But they weren't sad for long. A few days later Abunawas was smiling and walking outside the palace.

The emperor was furious and called for the guards to hang him at once. But after Abunawas had spoken, there was nothing the emperor could do but let him stay in Ethiopia and go wherever he wanted. How could this be?

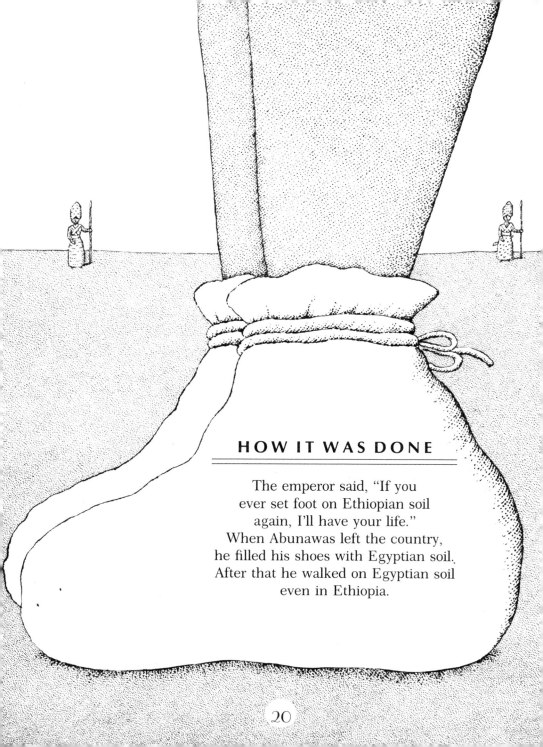

HOW IT WAS DONE

The emperor said, "If you
ever set foot on Ethiopian soil
again, I'll have your life."
When Abunawas left the country,
he filled his shoes with Egyptian soil.
After that he walked on Egyptian soil
even in Ethiopia.

4.

HEN'S OBSERVATION

One day Hen flew to the top of a giant stack of wheat to get some food and enjoy the view. When she saw Jackal coming near, she shook her head. He was always trying to eat her for lunch. Hen ignored him in hopes he'd go away.

"Good morning," called Jackal in his friendliest voice. "How are you this fine day?"

"Just fine," said Hen. She told him good-bye, but he stayed and stared.

"Hen," said Jackal. "Why don't you come closer to talk? Today is a special day of peace. Haven't you heard? All animals have agreed that no one may catch another today. It's perfectly safe."

"Are you sure?" asked Hen.

"Very sure," promised Jackal. "Come down and you'll see. We'll have a wonderful time."

After all the lies and tricks Jackal had tried in the past, Hen wasn't convinced she could trust him. As she stared across the surrounding field, Hen thought of a way to find out if Jackal was telling the truth.

"What are you staring at?" asked Jackal. "Come down and tell me."

Hen's answer not only proved that Jackal was lying about the animals making peace for a day, it also made him run off in fear, leaving Hen safe to finish her meal.

What could Hen have said?

HOW IT WAS DONE

Hen said, "A pack of big dogs is running this way."
Dogs are Jackal's natural enemies. If he'd been
telling the truth, Jackal would have had no reason
to run from the dogs.

5.
THE AGREEMENT

A merchant in the city of Bari once decided to go on a pilgrimage. Before going, he left his three hundred gold coins with his closest friend.

"If by chance I do not return," instructed the merchant, "give the money to the poor to pray for my soul. If I return, then give me back whatever you want and keep the rest for yourself."

When the merchant returned from his journey, he went to his friend and asked for his money back. The friend gave him ten coins.

"You're a thief!" yelled the merchant. "I gave you three hundred coins."

"I'm only doing what you told me to do," his friend explained. "You told me to give you back whatever I want, and I want to give you ten coins. You can take me to court if you like, but you know our agreement as well as I do."

26

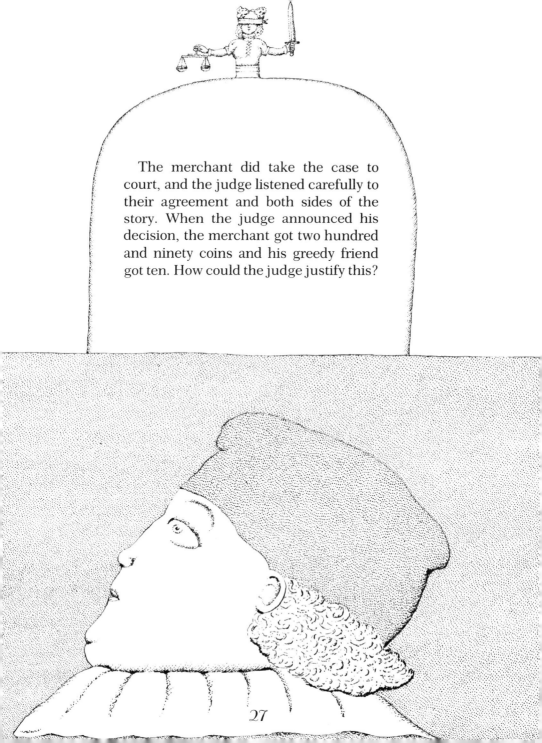

The merchant did take the case to court, and the judge listened carefully to their agreement and both sides of the story. When the judge announced his decision, the merchant got two hundred and ninety coins and his greedy friend got ten. How could the judge justify this?

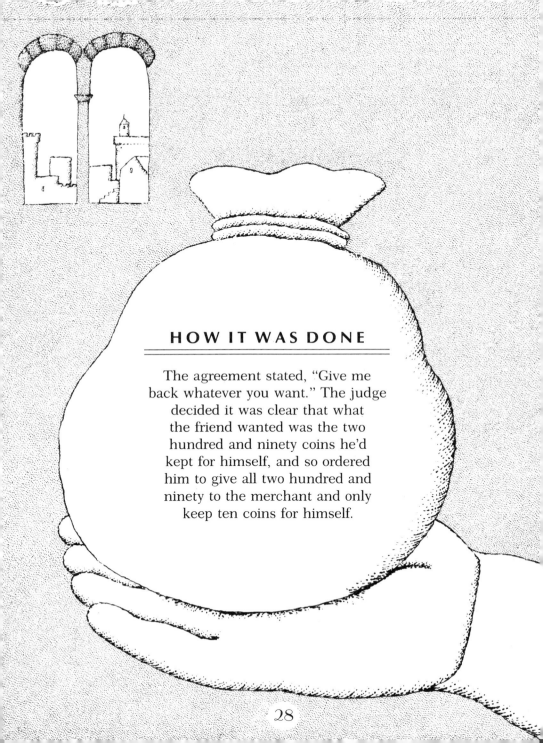

HOW IT WAS DONE

The agreement stated, "Give me back whatever you want." The judge decided it was clear that what the friend wanted was the two hundred and ninety coins he'd kept for himself, and so ordered him to give all two hundred and ninety to the merchant and only keep ten coins for himself.

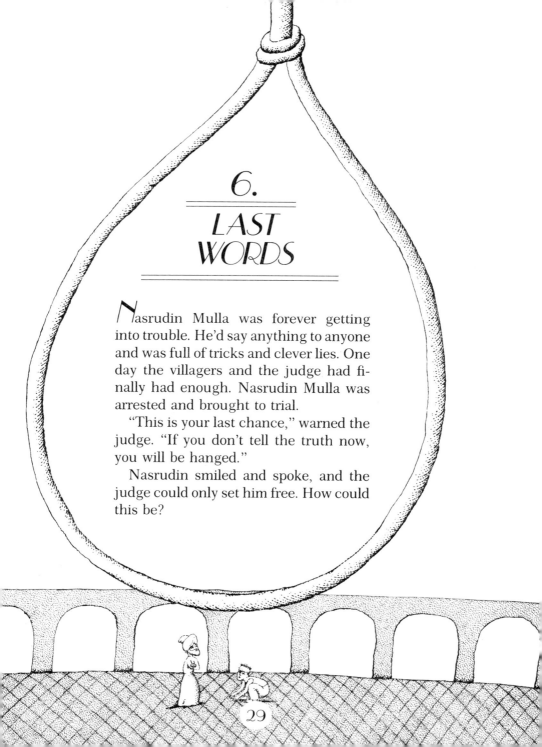

6.
LAST WORDS

Nasrudin Mulla was forever getting into trouble. He'd say anything to anyone and was full of tricks and clever lies. One day the villagers and the judge had finally had enough. Nasrudin Mulla was arrested and brought to trial.

"This is your last chance," warned the judge. "If you don't tell the truth now, you will be hanged."

Nasrudin smiled and spoke, and the judge could only set him free. How could this be?

HOW IT WAS DONE

Nasrudin Mulla said, "I am going to be hanged," which gave the judge a dilemma. If he *did* hang him, Nasrudin's statement would be true, which would mean he shouldn't have been hanged. But if he *didn't* hang him, it would mean Nasrudin had told another lie and should be hanged. But the judge couldn't do *that* without making Nasrudin's last words true. . . .
So the judge unhappily set him free.

7.
THE BASKET WEAVER

*L*ong ago there lived a king in Greece who loved to dress in disguise and visit the people of his kingdom. On one such visit he asked a basket weaver how much he earned.

"Only a coin a day," said the weaver. "With that I pay off an old debt, I invest in my future, and I feed eight mouths that live in my house."

The king couldn't imagine how the man did so much with just one coin a day. He finally gave in and asked what the weaver meant.

"I repay my old debt," explained the weaver, "to my parents for raising me by taking care of them now. I invest in the future by taking care of my own children so that they will take care of me in my old age. And when you count up my parents, four children, my wife, and myself, I have ___ eight mouths to feed."

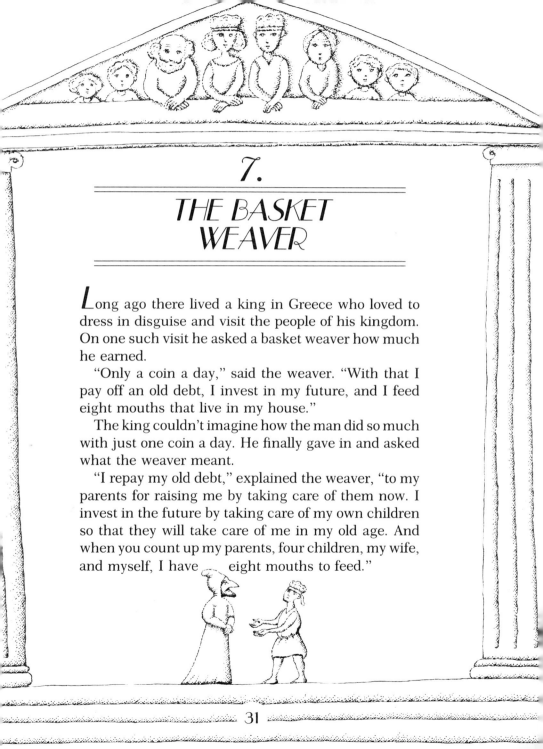

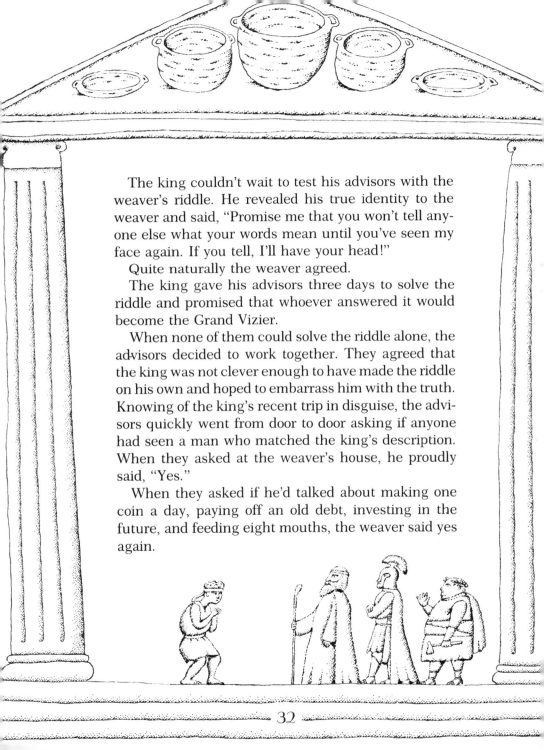

The king couldn't wait to test his advisors with the weaver's riddle. He revealed his true identity to the weaver and said, "Promise me that you won't tell anyone else what your words mean until you've seen my face again. If you tell, I'll have your head!"

Quite naturally the weaver agreed.

The king gave his advisors three days to solve the riddle and promised that whoever answered it would become the Grand Vizier.

When none of them could solve the riddle alone, the advisors decided to work together. They agreed that the king was not clever enough to have made the riddle on his own and hoped to embarrass him with the truth. Knowing of the king's recent trip in disguise, the advisors quickly went from door to door asking if anyone had seen a man who matched the king's description. When they asked at the weaver's house, he proudly said, "Yes."

When they asked if he'd talked about making one coin a day, paying off an old debt, investing in the future, and feeding eight mouths, the weaver said yes again.

"Then," ordered the advisors, "tell us what you mean."

The weaver explained that he couldn't. "I promised the king not to tell anyone."

The advisors were desperate. They offered him more and more money until it was finally so much he couldn't refuse. As soon as he told the advisors what his words really meant, they rushed back and told the king. He was furious and had guards drag the weaver to the palace.

"You promised to keep your riddle a secret till you saw my face again!" said the king. "And for breaking that promise I'll have your head."

"But I didn't break my promise," said the weaver.

"Yes, you did," said the king. "And now you're lying, on top of everything else."

"No, I'm not." And when the weaver explained, the king was so impressed he made the weaver his Grand Vizier. How did the weaver explain?

HOW IT WAS DONE

The weaver *had* seen the king's face.
It was on all the coins
the king's advisors had given him.

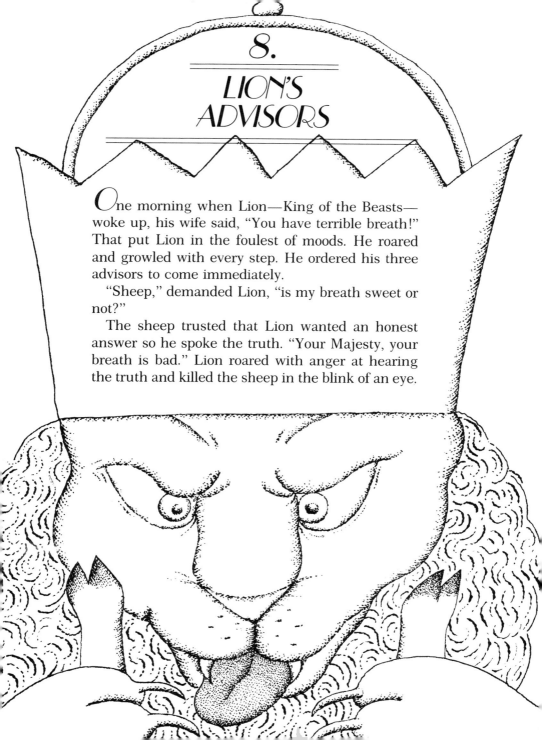

8.
LION'S ADVISORS

One morning when Lion—King of the Beasts—woke up, his wife said, "You have terrible breath!" That put Lion in the foulest of moods. He roared and growled with every step. He ordered his three advisors to come immediately.

"Sheep," demanded Lion, "is my breath sweet or not?"

The sheep trusted that Lion wanted an honest answer so he spoke the truth. "Your Majesty, your breath is bad." Lion roared with anger at hearing the truth and killed the sheep in the blink of an eye.

"Wolf," demanded Lion, "is my breath sweet or not?"

The wolf was well aware of what had just happened to the sheep. "Oh, yes, Your Majesty. Your breath is sweet—as sweet as the finest blossoms."

Lion roared with anger as he had before. "You're flattering me like a fool just to save your life, but it won't work!" He killed the wolf just as quickly as he had the sheep.

36

Now the fox was Lion's only advisor still alive.

"Fox," demanded Lion, "is my breath sweet or not?"

Fox coughed as he glanced at the bodies of the wolf and the sheep, then slowly gave his answer. Lion not only sent the fox home safe and alive, he even said he understood.

What did the fox say that not only got Lion to spare his life, but even got Lion's sympathy?

37

HOW IT WAS DONE

As the fox pretended to cough, he told Lion,
"I have such a terrible cold, I can't smell anything."

38

9.

A LESSON WELL LEARNED

There once lived a wise teacher in China who loved to retreat to a cave and read. Still, students frequently gathered at the cave, eager to learn new lessons. One day two students grew very tired of waiting.

"Master," they called, "it is long past time for our lesson."

The teacher smiled and said, "Your lesson for today is to see if you can find a way to get me to leave my comfortable cave."

39

The first student tried to convince the teacher that dragons that had to be seen to be believed were fighting on the other side of the hill. But the teacher didn't leave his cave. The second student cried out that the emperor's family was passing their way and that if they didn't run out and bow they'd be arrested. Once again the teacher refused to leave his cool, quiet cave. The two students tried and tried as best they could, but finally shook their heads.

"We've failed," said the first student. "There's no way we can get you to leave the cave."

"But wait," said the second. "I'm certain we can get you to do *this* instead."

As the student explained, the teacher hurriedly left his cave before he realized that he'd been fooled.

"It worked!" the student cheered. "We *did* get you to leave the cave."

"So you did," said the teacher, and praised the student for his cleverness.

What did the student say that made the teacher leave his cave?

HOW IT WAS DONE

The student said he was certain that
if the teacher was sitting outside the
cave, they could get him to go inside.
In order for the teacher to prove them
wrong, he had to leave the cave.

10.

A CLEVER SONG

There once lived a blind singer who went from town to town and fair to fair. Over the years he had managed to save a hundred gold coins. He kept them buried near an old oak tree in a meadow outside his hometown.

One day as he was digging by the tree to add more coins, a farmer saw him from a neighboring field.

The farmer was curious about what was going on, and as soon as the singer was gone the farmer ran over to see what he'd been digging. When he discovered the coins, the farmer danced for joy. He took them home and felt safe that a blind man could never figure out who had taken the coins.

When the singer returned the next day and found all his money gone, he cried, "Why did this happen to me?" There was nothing he could do except start saving all over again.

But that night the singer realized there *was* something he could do. The next day was the big market day when everyone came into town. He worked all night on a special song to sing.

The next morning the singer sang his new song and danced while everyone clapped and crowded around. They gave him many new coins, but best of all, his new song worked just as he had hoped it would. When he went back to the tree that evening the singer found that all his gold coins had been put back. He quickly gathered them up and hid them in a brand-new spot. What were the words that made the song work?

HOW IT WAS DONE

The song he sang
went like this:

"I've buried a hundred
coins by the tree,
And tonight I'll bury
that many more!"

When the greedy farmer
heard the song, he
wanted the new coins he
thought the singer was
going to bury later that
day. But he knew that
when the singer found
out his first hundred
coins were missing, he
wouldn't bury the second
hundred there. To be
sure of getting the
second hundred coins,
the farmer reburied the
coins he'd already stolen.

11.

THE
SECRET
SPEAR

One winter long ago, in the far north, the earth shook so violently that homes were destroyed. People ran for their lives as chunks of ice came crashing from the frozen sea. In the panic two people were left behind: a little boy and a shaman so old he'd lost most of his magic powers. The fish and animals had also fled, so there was nothing for the boy and shaman to eat. Their only hope was to walk over the mountains and fish in the bay of their enemy.

When they finally reached the other bay, the boy and shaman were very weak.

"Listen," said the shaman as the boy began to fish through the ice. "Our enemies will surely see us soon and try to kill us. They know my powers are gone, but you can make use of the secret spear. I'll teach you. They'll believe a boy as strong as you could have special powers."

The boy was afraid but said he'd do his best. Just then they saw two fierce-looking hunters charging their way. The shaman quickly told the boy the powerful words he needed to say in order to make the secret spear work.

The two hunters said they were going to kill the boy and old man, but the old man told them it would be impossible.

"The boy has a secret spear with magic powers," said the old shaman. "It can catch any game he hunts and protects us from every danger."

The hunters just laughed, but the shaman insisted, "No weapons you have can equal his!"

The proud hunters weren't about to let any child get the better of them. They ordered the boy to tell them the magic words that made his secret spear work. "Tell us *now* or we'll kill you and take your spear away."

The boy nervously agreed, but explained, "I can only tell you one at a time. That's part of how the magic works."

He whispered to one hunter and then the next. The two hunters stared at each other, then suddenly began to argue and fight. Within minutes they had stabbed each other to death and fallen through the fishing hole into the frigid sea.

When others from the enemy village came running up, they were awed. No one had come close to defeating even one of the two fierce hunters before. The villagers quickly agreed to let the old shaman and the boy fish in their bay as long as they needed.

What *was* the boy's secret spear? What were the magic words the old shaman told the boy to say?

HOW IT WAS DONE

Words were the secret spear. The magic words
the boy told the hunters weren't magic at all.
He simply said, "I can only tell the fiercest
hunter how my secret spear works." In trying
to prove which of them was the fiercer, the
two hunters ended up killing each other.

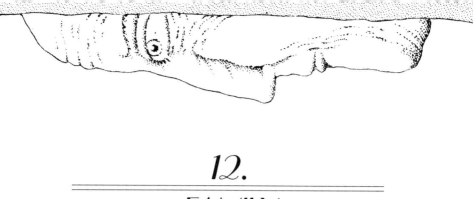

12.
FAMILY HISTORY

*L*ong ago there lived a poor family who struggled to care for themselves. The husband and wife worked hard every day, and their son was always busy doing errands. The grandfather, however, had gotten too old and weak to work. He needed constant attention and his hands shook so much he made a mess when he ate. The boy tried to feed his grandfather and shared his food with him, but his parents said it was a waste of good food. The grandfather was unhappy, but the young couple only scolded him when he complained.

Things eventually got so bad that the couple began to plan how they might get rid of the old man. They finally decided to take him far into the woods and leave him there. If he was found by others, he'd receive help. If not, he'd die. But they reasoned he was old anyway and only a burden.

The next morning the husband loaded his father into a large basket that he strapped to his back. The old man grumbled, and the little boy cried, "Where are you taking him? Does he have to go?"

"Oh, yes," said the man. "He's too old and needs to be taken to a special place where he'll get more attention. Understand?"

The boy said, "Yes."

And then, with only love in his heart for his father, the boy asked one favor. His request made his father's legs go weak, and he brought the old man back to the house. What favor did the boy ask?

HOW IT WAS DONE

He asked his father to bring the empty basket back home so that he would be able to take him— his own father—away to such a special place when he got too old to work.

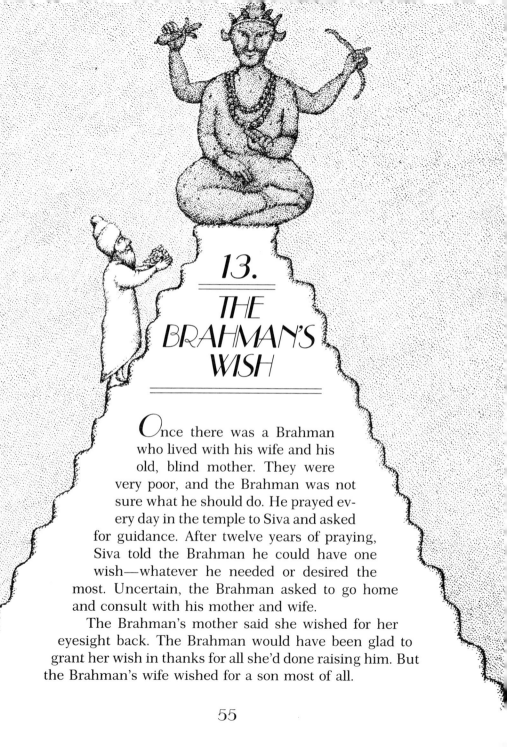

13.

THE BRAHMAN'S WISH

Once there was a Brahman who lived with his wife and his old, blind mother. They were very poor, and the Brahman was not sure what he should do. He prayed every day in the temple to Siva and asked for guidance. After twelve years of praying, Siva told the Brahman he could have one wish—whatever he needed or desired the most. Uncertain, the Brahman asked to go home and consult with his mother and wife.

The Brahman's mother said she wished for her eyesight back. The Brahman would have been glad to grant her wish in thanks for all she'd done raising him. But the Brahman's wife wished for a son most of all.

"Your mother is old, with little time to see," said the wife. "But a son could take care of us when we are old."

The poor Brahman didn't know what to do. He didn't want to say no to either one. He walked and cried and cried and walked till he finally sat down in the center of town. Many people passed by before a sergeant stopped and asked, "What's wrong?"

The Brahman told him how after praying to Siva for twelve years he had been granted only one wish.

"But my mother wants one thing," he explained. "And my wife wants another. How can I choose whose wish to fulfill? I love them both."

The sergeant smiled and said, "No need to cry. Your problem is small." Then he told the Brahman exactly what to do.

When the Brahman returned to Siva the next day, both his mother and his wife had their wishes fulfilled. What had the sergeant told him to do and say?

HOW IT WAS DONE

The sergeant advised him to combine the two wishes in one. When the Brahman went to Siva, he said, "My mother is blind, and her only desire is to see her grandson eating his rice."

14.
A HANDFUL OF MUSTARD SEED

A young woman gave birth to a son, and like all parents she and her husband loved their baby more than words could tell. Then tragedy came. Before their son was a year old, he became very ill and died. The mother cried for days, refusing to let anyone bury her child. She begged everyone to help her find some kind of medicine that would bring her son to life again.

Many people thought she'd gone mad, but a wise man told her to go ask Buddha.

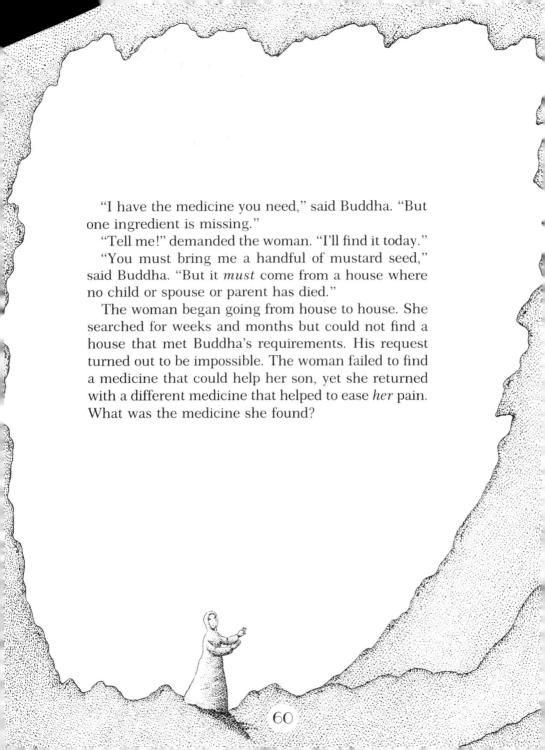

"I have the medicine you need," said Buddha. "But one ingredient is missing."

"Tell me!" demanded the woman. "I'll find it today."

"You must bring me a handful of mustard seed," said Buddha. "But it *must* come from a house where no child or spouse or parent has died."

The woman began going from house to house. She searched for weeks and months but could not find a house that met Buddha's requirements. His request turned out to be impossible. The woman failed to find a medicine that could help her son, yet she returned with a different medicine that helped to ease *her* pain. What was the medicine she found?

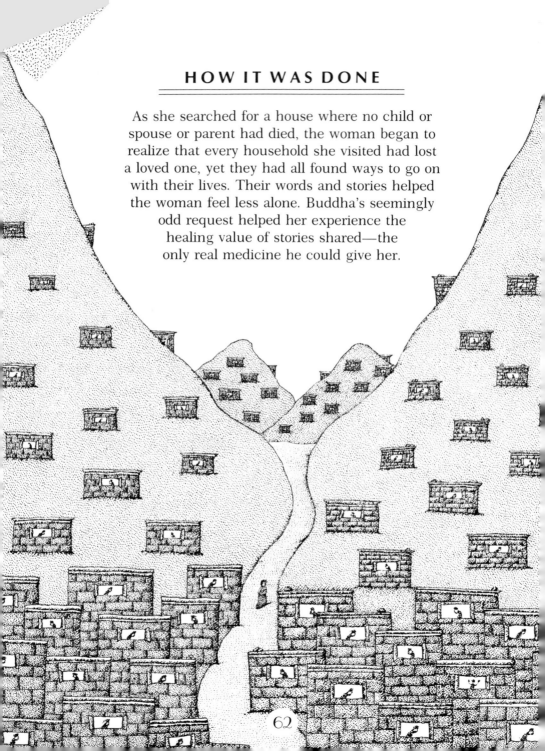

HOW IT WAS DONE

As she searched for a house where no child or
spouse or parent had died, the woman began to
realize that every household she visited had lost
a loved one, yet they had all found ways to go on
with their lives. Their words and stories helped
the woman feel less alone. Buddha's seemingly
odd request helped her experience the
healing value of stories shared—the
only real medicine he could give her.

NOTES

1. THE LINE is an Urdu folktale from central India. It is retold from *Folktales from India: A Selection of Oral Tales from Twenty-two Languages*, selected and edited by A. K. Ramanujan (Pantheon, 1991). Ramanujan worked from Frances Pritchett's translations of Mhanarayan, *Lata'if-e Akbar, Hissah Pahla: Birbal Namah* (Delhi, 1888).

2. TWO HORSES is retold from *Jewish Folktales*, selected and retold by Pinhas Sadeh and translated from the Hebrew by Hillel Halkin (Doubleday, 1989). When Sadeh collected this tale, it was already told as a riddle story. Tales in which sons compete for their father's inheritance are told in many cultures. Examples can be found in "The Three Brothers" in *The Complete Grimm's Fairy Tales* and "The Cleverest Son" in my *Stories to Solve*.

3. NEVER SET FOOT is a Somali-Ethiopian folktale. It is retold from *The Fire on the Mountain and Other Ethiopian Stories* by Harold Courlander and Wolf Lesau (Holt, 1950). Variants can be found in many cultures, including Haitian, Italian, and Danish, and among the Tagalog of the Philippines and the Maliseet and Appalachian peoples of North America.

4. HEN'S OBSERVATION is retold from *Tales from Basotho*, collected by Minnie Postma and translated from Afrikaans by Susie McDermid (University of Texas Press, 1974). Variations of this tale can be found in the classic collections *Aesop's Fables* and *1,001 Nights* as well as in cultures ranging from Cambodian to Scottish to Russian to Uruguayan, and among the Huron-Wyandot of North America.

5. THE AGREEMENT is an Italian folktale. It is retold from *Old Italian Tales*, retold by Domenico Vittorini (McKay, 1958), and *The Disobedient Eels and Other Italian Tales* by Maria Cimino (Pantheon, 1970). A variant also appeared in *The United States Almanac for 1800* (Shepard Kollock).

6. LAST WORDS is retold from *The Incomparable Exploits of Mulla Nasrudin*, edited by Indries Shah (Dutton, 1972). Shah gives no sources. A seemingly endless number of tales recount the foolishness and clever tricks of the Middle Eastern folk hero known as Hoja or Nasreddin.

7. THE BASKET WEAVER is retold from *Folktales of Greece*, edited by Georgios A. Megas and translated by Helen Colaclides (University of Chicago Press, 1970). Megas's source was collected by S. Sathis in 1909. Variants can be found in Hungary, India, Italy, Latvia, the Cape Verde Islands, and sections of East Africa.

8. LION'S ADVISORS is one of Aesop's ancient fables. A Burmese variant can be found in *The Tiger's Whisker and Other Tales and Legends from Asia and the Pacific* by Harold Courlander (Harcourt, 1959). Spanish and Jewish variants also exist.

9. A LESSON WELL LEARNED is a Chinese folktale. It is retold from *Pebbles from a Broken Jar: Fables and Hero Stories from Old China*, retold by Frances Alexander (Bobbs-Merrill, 1963), and *Folk Tales from China* by Lim Sian-tek (John Day, 1944), who researched ancient Chinese books.

10. A CLEVER SONG is an Italian folktale. It is retold from *The Fairy Tale Tree: Stories from All Over the World*, retold by Vladislav Stanovsky and Jan Vladislav and translated by Jean Layton (Putnam, 1961). The tale can also be found in Spanish, Japanese, and Egyptian collections. A variant attributing the clever method of retrieving stolen gold to King Solomon can be found in *Ma'aseh Book*, Volume II, by Moses Gaster (Jewish Publication Society of America, 1934).

11. THE SECRET SPEAR is retold from "Agayk and the Strangest Spear" in *Trickster Tales* by I. G. Edmonds (Lippincott, 1966). Edmonds gives no sources. I have not been able to find a second source, and some experts think it is not an Inuit tale at all. The folklore of the Inuit peoples of the Arctic (known to many as Eskimos) *is*, however, filled with tales of powerful shamans and their magical powers. Related tales that involve winning by getting one's competition to cancel out one another can be found in China, Madagascar, and among the Assiniboin and Ojibwa peoples of North America.

12. FAMILY HISTORY is a Nepalese tale retold from *Folk Tales from Asia for Children Everywhere: Book Four* by the Asian Cultural Centre for UNESCO (Weatherhill, 1976). Variants can be found throughout Asia and Europe, including *The Complete Grimm's Fairy Tales*.

13. THE BRAHMAN'S WISH is a West Indian tale retold from *Folktales Told Around the World*, edited by Richard Dorson (University of Chicago Press, 1975). Daniel J. Crowley collected this tale in Curepe, Trinidad, and first published it in the September 1955 issue of *The Caribbean*.

14. A HANDFUL OF MUSTARD SEED is a Buddhist story retold from *Popular Tales and Fictions: Their Migrations and Transformations*, Volume II, by W. A. Clouston (London: Blackwood, 1887). Clouston worked from *Buddhaghosha's Parables*, translated from the Burmese by Henry Thomas Rogers (London: Trubner, 1870). The Greek satirist Lucien included a variant in "Demonax," written in the second century A.D.